THE STEP CHILDREN

Oregon Trail Series Book 2

KATIE WYATT

RoyceCardiff
Publishing House
WHOLESOME INSPIRATIONAL ROMANCE

RoyceCardiff
Publishing House
WHOLESOME INSPIRATIONAL ROMANCE

Dear Reader,

It is our utmost pleasure and privilege to bring these wonderful stories to you. I am so very proud of our amazing team of writers and the delight they continually bring us all with their beautiful clean and wholesome tales of, faith, courage, and love.

What is a book's lone purpose if not to be read and enjoyed? Therefore, you, dear reader, are the key to fulfilling that purpose and unlocking the treasures that lie within the pages of this book.

THANK YOU FOR CHOOSING A INSPIRATIONAL READS BY ROYCE CARDIFF PUBLISHING HOUSE.

Welcome and Enjoy!

CONTENTS

A PERSONAL WORD FROM KATIE

I LOVE WRITING ABOUT THE OLD WEST AND THE TRIALS, tribulations, and triumphs of the early pioneer women.

With strong fortitude and willpower, they took a big leap of faith believing in the promised land of the West. It was always not a bed of roses, however many found true love.

Most of the stories are based on some historical fact or personal conversations I've had with folks who knew something of that time. For example a relative of the Wyatt Earp's. I have spent much time out in the West camping hiking and carousing. I have spent countless hours gazing up at night thinking of how it must been back then.

Thank you for being a loyal reader.

Katie

KATIE WYATT

OREGON TRAIL SERIES.

A PERSONAL WORD FROM KATIE

I LOVE WRITING ABOUT THE OLD WEST AND THE TRIALS, tribulations, and triumphs of the early pioneer women.

With strong fortitude and willpower, they took a big leap of faith believing in the promised land of the West. It was always not a bed of roses, however many found true love.

Most of the stories are based on some historical fact or personal conversations I've had with folks who knew something of that time. For example a relative of the Wyatt Earp's. I have spent much time out in the West camping hiking and carousing. I have spent countless hours gazing up at night thinking of how it must been back then.

Thank you for being a loyal reader.

Katie

KATIE WYATT

OREGON TRAIL SERIES.

CHAPTER 1
JANUARY 28TH, 1850

GUTHRIE, OKLAHOMA

MY WEDDING DAY WAS, QUITE POSSIBLY, THE WORST DAY of my life. Of course, the days my parents and my grand-mother, who subsequently raised me, died were all contenders. The day only a few weeks back where I'd realized I had to leave my home in Raleigh, North Carolina, had been horrible, too. That painful chapter of my life was still all too fresh. Still, this day was even worse than any of those days. Perhaps it was the finality of saying vows to a man I didn't know that was so overwhelmingly painful. Though, I suspected that the fact that I was in love with someone else was contributing greatly to the ache in my heart and the churning of my stomach. As I stood holding hands with a perfect stranger, feeling that I should listen to the preacher's words but knowing I didn't care, I tried to name all the emotions I was experiencing.

There was exhaustion, for one thing. I'd ridden on a train for three days before stepping onto the platform here and being whisked off to be married. My neck seemed to have a permanent crick in it and I was desperate for a bath or change of clothing. I also felt as though I was in someone else's life. Surely I wasn't marrying James Tucker, farmer and very serious man. I prided myself on my mastery of the flirtatious arts and I had yet to figure out a way to successfully charm serious men. But then, was a woman supposed to flirt with her husband? That didn't seem appropriate somehow, much to my disappointment.

I peeked around James' imposing form and spotted his three children standing close behind him. The oldest daughter, Emma, was nine years old and, if I was any judge of character, hated me with all her being. This was especially impressive since we'd only known each other for about a half of an hour and had yet to exchange words. Three-year-old Lucy was squirming and seemed to be singing a song to her fingers under her breath. As for two-year-old Joseph, he was mostly busy picking his nose and staring out the windows.

I'd never desired becoming a mother. Never. I couldn't even think of the last time I'd been forced to interact with a child. My friends back in Raleigh were all unmarried women who worked in local shops. So, added in to the exhaustion and complete strangeness I was experiencing, there was also the dread of having to deal with children, as well as my frank terror of them. Why hadn't the marriage broker, Mr. Wainwright, thought to tell me that the man he was sending me to marry had children? I'd have liked to go back to his tiny office and give him a piece of my mind.

I sighed to myself. The other options that he had offered hadn't been any better. Even if I'd known about these additions to my potential husband, I probably would have ended up choosing him anyway. Oh, yes, I was feeling quite defeated.

But more than any of that, I was heartbroken. On the train during the past few days, I'd met a handsome soldier by the name of Simon Hart who had completely won me over. He was dashing and funny and charming and everything I thought made an ideal man. Unfortunately, he was headed off to Fort Laramie in Wyoming, under strict orders from the U.S. Army, and I had signed a contract to marry James Tucker. Despite our chemistry and mutual attraction, we were star-crossed lovers. And by lovers, I mean two people who knew each other as well as three days on a train would allow, who had also spent some time kissing in a dark storage car.

Now, as I looked up at the man who was almost my husband, I tried to gauge how guilty I felt about that kissing. My conscience didn't even offer up a whimper. I was glad I'd kissed Simon. No matter how disappointing my life with the Tuckers became, I would always have the memories of that soldier to remind me that I'd once been young and pretty.

"Do you, Betsy Bradley, take this man to be your lawfully wedded husband?" The preacher wheezed, his wide eyes staring over his spectacles at me, awaiting my response.

No, I didn't. I didn't want to marry the serious James Tucker. I wanted to run away. But I had no money, no family, and no job skills. I didn't have much of a choice.

"I do," I said, and tried to arrange my face so that I looked like I wasn't contemplating turning and bolting for the door.

After that, I stopped listening altogether, though I'm pretty sure that James agreed to marry me in return. The preacher's voice came to an end and he started shaking James' hand and clapping him on the back. Then we were signing our names to a marriage license and walking back to the wagon.

Before I knew what was happening, the whole family was piling into the well-worn farm wagon and we were jostling off towards the endless prairie. It felt funny to think that I was now legally bound to this man and these children. We were on our way "home," whatever that might mean.

"It's about an hour's ride to the farm from Guthrie," James said into the silence that stretched between us.

"I see," I replied lamely. Our words abandoned us and I couldn't help but compare how different this was from when I'd first met Simon. We'd been strangers, too, but it hadn't been difficult or awkward. Conversation had easily sprung up between us and we'd hardly taken a breath for the entire first day we were together.

Before we'd gotten too far out of town, little Lucy popped her head up between us and said, "Papa? I have to go."

It was the closest I'd been to the girl and I noticed, for the first time, that she was slightly cross eyed. I sighed inwardly, refusing to allow myself to be won over by the cuteness of this small child. I stubbornly refused to let my heart warm towards this family. For some reason I couldn't name, it was important that I stay aloof and a little bit angry about the situation, at least for a little while longer.

"Do you mind?" James asked and I looked around to see who he was talking to. "Well, do you?" he prodded.

Oh, no, he was talking to me!

I looked down at Lucy as though she was a venomous spider asking to be taken for a walk. *Calm down, Betsy,* I tried to calm myself. This was a three-year-old child. How hard could it be to help her answer nature's call?

"Of course not," I finally replied, as though I did this sort of thing all the time.

The wagon pulled to a stop and James came around to help me down. Then he reached up and swung down his daughter, followed by his other two children.

"Erm, this way," I said, after assessing the rolling plains all around us. There wasn't a tree or bush in sight, just tall grass waving in the breeze. Well, it was only her family. Surely there wasn't much point in privacy.

We walked into the grass a little and I held down some of the tall stalks so that they wouldn't spring up while she was taking care of her business. Lucy looked up at me and wrinkled her nose.

"Get to it," I advised. "Your father wants to keep moving."

She lifted her skirt and dropped her cotton drawers and I helped her crouch down, then looked away, glad that none of my friends back home could see me now. Once Lucy had finished, Joseph needed to "go." I was on the verge of panicking, when James offered to take the boy. I wasn't sure that I could handle dealing with a little boy's bathroom needs on this already terrible day.

Eying Emma, I weighed the risks involved in actually speaking to her. It was tempting to ignore her glares and obviously angry posture. Still, James wouldn't be too happy to have to stop ten minutes down the road because his older daughter hadn't taken care of things when we'd stopped.

"Do you need help?" I asked warily.

Her hands went to her hips and Emma glared even harder, if that was possible. "I'm not a baby. I can take care of myself."

I opened my mouth to say something motherly, though I'm not sure what that would have been, when Lucy piped up in a very hurt voice.

"I'm not a baby!"

"You can't go by yourself. That's what babies do," Emma sneered, turning her considerable disapproval on her sister.

"No, I'm not!" Lucy wailed.

Good gracious! I gritted my teeth and prayed that this bickering was unusual and not going to be a common occurrence in the foreseeable future.

"Lucy, you're not a baby. Asking for help is a very grown up thing to do." I reached down and petted her hair awkwardly. "And, Emma, your father will be back any minute. I don't know if he'll be willing to stop again before we get home and that's almost an hour away. You should probably think about whether or not you can wait that long."

Emma chewed that over before turning and stomping off, her younger sister right behind her.

I leaned back against the wagon and hoped, not for the first time, that this was all a nightmare and I would soon wake to find that I wasn't in the middle of nowhere having irrevocably attached my life to that of this family. It was only too real, as I knew when shouts of anger came from the tall grass where the two girls had disappeared.

I copied my stepdaughter as I stomped off to collect the girls. Lucy wanted to stay with Emma, who wanted to be left alone. I tried coercing the little girl to come with me. I tried reasoning with her. Finally, I grabbed her by the arm and dragged her away. At least I was bigger and stronger. For now.

Without a word of thanks, James swung us all back up into the wagon and off we drove. I had to satisfy myself with being grateful that it wasn't cold and snowy. What would we have done if it had been ice cold out here when the girls needed to relieve themselves? I shuddered contemplating that fight and pulled my old coat around myself, regretting not having something warmer to wear.

"I guess you should know a little about us," James said after turning around and threatening the children with a formidable glare of his own. Now I knew where Emma got that particular trait from. "My ... first wife, Dorothy, and I came here when Emma was little and took up a homestead. It'll be seven years next month, which means that it'll be mine ... ours ... free and clear. That was always Dorothy's dream for us."

Compassion began to send up a tiny shoot inside me. I hadn't really considered that this family had lost a wife and mother. Having lost my own mother as a girl, I knew how hard that was.

"I'm sorry about your wife," I said quietly. "Has she been gone long?"

James swallowed hard and looked fixedly ahead. "Almost a year now."

The shoot of compassion opened up into a tiny bud in my heart. I couldn't imagine what it would take for a man to lose his wife and have the courage to contact a marriage broker to find him a new one so soon after that loss. As a farmer, though, I knew he would need to have someone to watch his children and keep his house. It was the sort of decision a person made with his head, while roundly ignoring his aching heart. For the first time, I wanted to help the Tuckers. I resolved to do what I could to help make things easier.

That resolution lasted the rest of the drive. It stayed strong despite bickering from the children and stilted conversation with their father. I was starting to feel rather self righteous about my saintly new frame of mind when James pulled up the wagon in the middle of a stretch of prairie.

"We're home," he said.

I looked around me, dread growing. Where was the house?

James caught my searching eyes and said, "There's not much wood out here for building houses. We've got a temporary soddy built."

A soddy? Tell me that wasn't what it sounded like.

CHAPTER 2

THE HOUSE ITSELF PROTRUDED FROM THE VERY SIDE OF the hill. The front was built of rough logs and sported a lone window, covered in what looked like oiled paper. The front door seemed sturdy enough, I was relieved to see. However, the top of the house was covered in sod and almost appeared to melt back into the hill. Even though it was late winter, there was no snow in sight. Everything was gray and dead. The grass on the top of the house was a brownish gray and matted. It was the most depressing homecoming I could imagine.

James pulled the wagon to a stop near the door and the children exploded from the back. I didn't want to leave the relative comfort of the hard board seat my bottom had been complaining about for the past twenty minutes or so. Having to go inside that ... dwelling was quite the most awful thing I'd ever been expected to do. Even mothering three small children in various stages of resentment was less intimidating than walking into what was sure to be an uncomfortable hut and then living there for the foreseeable future. Why hadn't I gone on with Simon? Living in an army barracks with a dozen men seemed glamorous compared to this.

Since my new husband was busy corralling his children and wrestling my trunk back out of the wagon, I was left to climb down on my own. I was much more familiar with buggies and couldn't remember the last time I'd ridden in an honest-to-goodness farm wagon. The wheels were placed exactly in the wrong place for a woman wearing long skirts and attractive, if a bit worn, boots with a small heel. It took me almost a full minute to get my skirts modestly collected in one hand, find a good handhold with the other, and carefully step over the side and down onto the wheel before attempting to find the ground. In fact, the entire family had been herded into the soddy before I was steady on my feet.

"Welcome home," I grumbled to myself under my breath as I steeled myself and entered the house.

The floor was packed earth, with not a board or rug to disguise that fact. The walls, which I expected to be bare earth as well, were made of bricks. All four walls were bricked in from floor to ceiling, with the exception of the one window and the door. This seemed very practical, though not very attractive, since it would hold in heat in the winter and cool air from the ground in the summer. Two sturdy beams supported the ceiling, I was glad to see. Wooden rafters ran every few feet and between them I could see the underside of the sod. How was a woman expected to keep a clean house when the floor and the ceiling were made of dirt?

James lit a lantern and the light filled the corners as well as it could manage. I took in an old cast iron cook stove whose exhaust vent reached up through the ceiling. There was a rough table and two benches on either side near the stove. A bucket sat near the door and a porcelain basin (the only decorative item in the house) perched on a wooden stand under the window. A bed that seemed far too narrow for two adults who were mostly still strangers, a rickety chest of drawers, a small set of cupboards, and a straw tick supporting a pile of quilts and blankets rounded out the furniture that belonged to the James Tucker family.

My heart sank and I wanted to cry. This seemed like too cruel a punishment for the mere crime of almost kissing a married man. What had I done to deserve this?

It would have been easy to give in to my tears and throw a full-blown tantrum. However, James muttered something about preparing supper and needing to put the animals in the barn. Since his statement was quickly followed by his exit, I supposed that meant that I was in charge of supper.

Which meant that we were in a pickle. Now, don't get me wrong, I can cook. A few things, that is. I can fry bacon and make pancakes. My grandmother insisted I learn how to make bread as a girl, though I hadn't attempted the task for several years now. I could follow a recipe if I had one and was usually moderately successful. Cooking hadn't come to my mind when I'd imagined myself in my new life. Then again, most of those imaginings had most recently involved Corporal Simon Hart and the adorable cabin we'd have out in the wilds of Wyoming.

Cries of displeasure broke into my misery and I pulled Emma and Joseph—who were aggravating one another—apart. Lucy began to wail that she wanted to go with her father to the barn. I was quite sure that he did not want his daughter getting underfoot, so that was quite out of the question. There were three crying children and supper to be prepared.

I pulled myself up to my full five feet and two inches and announced, "It's time to get supper ready! Who wants to help?"

Emma glared at me. Joseph put one chubby finger up his nose. Lucy stopped wailing and raised a hand.

We were off to a fantastic start.

Lucy proved to be helpful, though she was easily distracted and was soon off singing to her fingers, once again, in the corner. Before she abandoned me for her imaginary world, she pointed out the stores, kept in a small lean-to on the side of the house, and where the woodpile could be found.

The wood in the stove had burned down to embers, but there were still some alight, thank goodness. I didn't know how strong my fire-making abilities were, having never had to try them out. All I had to do on this occasion was add a few logs and branches to the belly of the stove and wait for it to produce heat.

"Don't let the little ones touch the stove," I advised Emma.

"They already know not to do that. They're not stupid."

Ah, her first words to me. I would treasure them always.

I wrapped my arms around myself and went back out to the lean-to, glad to be alone for a few moments at least. The outdoor pantry was well stocked. There was a large supply of flour, lard, and potatoes. A string of onions hung from the rafters, kept company by a large side of beef and some herbs I didn't recognize. After poking around a bit, I discovered evidence of a recent hog butchering, in the form of two good-sized hams and bacon.

It took me two trips to haul enough potatoes, onions, and one of the hams back to the house, where I struggled to cut off two thick slices before lugging the remainder back to the pantry. While I was engaged in these activities, I broke up another argument, told Lucy to stop climbing on the table, and was followed about with a now-whining Joseph.

Cooking over a fire was never an exact science. Whether it was a cast iron stove like this one or a fireplace, regulating the temperature was always a challenge. Experienced cooks got a feel for how a stove cooked and what the coals should look like. I did not have this skill as yet and spent a fair bit of time adding more wood and then sweating in the ensuing swell of heat. I cut up the potatoes and fried them with an onion in the one wide pan I could find. Once that was done, I moved the potatoes to the warming oven on the back of the stove, rinsed the pan, and put the first of the ham slices in to cook in water. Meanwhile, the whirling dervish of childish mischief raged around me.

By the time that James came in expecting supper, there were only a few more minutes before the second ham slice was cooked. He carried a pail of milk, which he set down on the table.

"I brought you some milk," he said, then waited for me to say something.

I had no idea what response he expected. "What do you want me to do with it?" I finally said, too tired to think any more.

James looked mildly irritated by this question. "The children drink milk with their meals. The rest you can use to make butter or cheese."

I tried not to, but I couldn't help myself and rolled my eyes. "Do you expect me to make butter tonight?"

"Have you ever made butter before?" he shot back at me, seeming to loom over me from his great height.

"Not once." It was childishly satisfying to admit it. "I haven't the faintest idea how to cook most things."

At that point, Lucy climbed on the table and stuck her finger in the milk. James turned to her and snapped, "Get your hand out of there, girl! That's disgusting."

To which the three-year-old burst into surprised and hurt tears, wailing loud enough to be heard back in Guthrie. Not to be left out, Joseph began to cry too, for no particular reason.

I turned back to finishing supper preparations and allowed my new husband to deal with the mess that was his children. In less than five minutes the food was dished up and we were all sitting around the table. Apparently, my cooking was acceptable. Though it received no compliments, there were also no complaints.

Mostly, we chewed in silence. Emma tried to tattle on her sister at one point, but a stern look from her father and that came to a quick halt. I tried to think of something to talk about with James, but I knew so little about him that I couldn't think of anything. The weather was gray, but was that normal or unusual for these parts? The president was making a mess of things, but had James voted for him or not? The children were hideous, but since they were his, I didn't think it was wise to point out that their table manners left something to be desired.

A sense of overwhelming sadness rose up in me. I tried to ignore it, to chalk it up to being tired and hungry, to busy myself with cleaning up supper. Once I lay in bed for the night on the edge of the small bed with Lucy in the middle and Emma pushed up against the wall, I couldn't ignore it any more. James and Joseph shared the straw tick on the floor, for which I was relieved. If I'd had to share this narrow mattress with that man, I would have died of embarrassment.

As James's snores took on a steady rhythm and Lucy's little teeth knocked together occasionally in her sleep, I allowed myself a few silent tears. All the way here on the train I'd been able to put off thinking about the reality of what my new life would be. There were so many possibilities that it hadn't borne considering. Now I was locked into this one reality and I couldn't pretend anymore. I was married to a tall, quiet man who had three rambunctious children. My home was a soddy in the middle of the prairie with a dirt floor. Tomorrow would be another day filled with breaking up arguments and trying to think of interesting things to make with the same few ingredients. The next day would be the same, and so would the one after that and the one after that.

There were no more supper parties for me. No more dates or flirting or fun. There weren't even any books to read in this house. I would work my fingers to the bone as a servant girl for this family until the day I died. Was there any chance that James would ever warm up to me? The thought of kissing him was absurd. He simply wasn't the kissing type. There was nothing remotely romantic about him.

I wiped away my tears and took a few shuddering breaths as quietly as I could. Then I relived every moment on the train with Simon Hart. I fell asleep just as I was remembering our sweet goodbye.

CHAPTER 3

I WAS AWAKENED BEFORE THE SUN CAME UP BY LUCY, who needed the outhouse. Groggily, I pulled on my shoes, found her boots, and stumbled outside into the cold to help her. The family did keep a chamber pot inside, but Lucy insisted that it was "icky" and refused to use it. The gray sky hadn't changed at all since the previous day, but the air felt crisper and the wind had a bite to it. By the time we got back inside, I was shivering and alert.

The day ahead was weighing heavily on me and I wasn't sure what I could do to make it better than the one before. This family was sure to have routines and ways of doing things that I would need to learn. It was possible that James was the sort of man who felt that the house and its running belonged to the woman and would leave us alone. Of course, he might be the sort who wanted everything done a particular way and would resent changes. I didn't know. I also had no idea what time it was. When would he wake up? Should I build up the fire? We were all snuggled under piles of worn quilts and blankets with ragged edges, but I could see my breath and knew that the children would be much happier to wake up to a warmer temperature outside their beds.

After hemming and hawing for a long time, I finally slid out from my warm spot in bed and went out to the wood-pile to get a few logs. Despite the cold air inside the house, it was much colder outside and I was wearing only my nightgown, stockings, boots, and a shawl. I scurried back into the relative warmth and built up the fire in the stove. Then I eased myself back into bed, where I drifted off into a shallow sleep.

The sounds of the door closing woke me not long after and I looked over to see that James had left. His clothes were absent from the hooks on the wall and I was relieved that he'd dressed while I was asleep. Not knowing how long he'd be away, I threw on my clothes and then started breakfast. It was much easier to fix this meal than the previous one, since the children were still in bed, though by the end of my preparations, their little voices were sounding from the mounds that remained in the beds.

"Do you want to get in bed with your sisters?" I asked Joseph when he began to get fussy. He nodded sleepily and I turned to where Lucy's face was barely visible. "I'm going to bring him over as fast I can. Will you lift the blankets as soon as we get there?"

Lucy's eyes twinkled, and I thought I saw her nod. I returned the nod and said, "Ready, Joseph? One, two, three!" On the count of three, I threw back his covers, pulled him from the bed, whirled around and called, "Now, Lucy!"

That little stinker shook her head, giggling, and refused to throw back the blankets. Joseph's face was still alight with the excitement of being whisked from his bed. To salvage the moment, I let out a howl of pretend frustration and begged, "Please, Lucy! Please let Joseph in! We're freezing out here!"

"Fweezing," the two-year-old echoed with another giggle.

His sister considered for a moment before throwing the heavy pile of blankets back as far as she could manage. I reached out to clear the path and deposited my wriggling bundle on the bed. Cheers were given all around and I tucked the blankets snugly back around them.

"You three stay nice and toasty in there until breakfast is ready." I put my hand on my hip and shook my other hand at them in mock sternness. "No tickles and no giggles in there. I mean it!"

A round of laughter answered my call and I went to check and see if the egg dish I'd invented was cooked through. It need a few more minutes, so I found the children's clothes and handed them to the three giggly, tickling creatures in the bed to warm up. I was feeling proud of myself for handling the morning so well until my husband arrived with another pail of milk and a blast of cold air.

"Why aren't the children up and dressed yet?"

He hadn't even bothered to say good morning, which changed my mood from happy to grumpy in an instant.

"It's cold out still and I thought they could stay warm under the covers until breakfast was closer to being ready."

"It isn't ready yet?"

I could have cheerfully hit him over the head with his pail of milk. Without waiting for a reply, James began barking at the children to get up and dressed. All the giggles and silliness evaporated and the tickling turned to crying and arguing.

It was becoming painfully obvious that I was not married to a man who exercised patience with his children. I wondered about this as I set the table and poured milk for us all. Were the children crying and angry because their father treated them gruffly? It would be difficult to raise children and cook their meals, all while running a farm. At the end of the day he was sure to have little energy left for whimsy. I determined to help make this a happier home. Perhaps I wasn't the best cook and I didn't really know much about children, but I was an expert in having fun, and that gift I would gladly contribute to this family's well being.

Once we were settled and Grace was said, I turned to my husband. "James, what it is that you need me to do today? I've never lived on a farm before. When would you like lunch prepared? Are there any chores that need doing?"

He looked up at me from behind his bushy blond eyebrows, brown eyes unreadable. "Call me Jim."

Well, that wasn't a good sign. We'd been married almost an entire day before I knew my own husband's preferred name. If I needed further evidence that my marriage was off to a rocky start, here it was.

"I'll be working on bringing in the last of the winter wheat today. You can send Emma out with something around noon."

"Does she know where you'll be?" It made sense to me that it would be obvious where he was, since there were no trees to block the view, but I wanted to be certain. I didn't expect Jim to handle having to wait for his lunch well.

"North pasture," was the short reply.

I glanced at Emma, who nodded obediently at her father before scowling at me. I sighed. "Is there washing to do? A creek nearby?"

Jim thought this over. "It's too cold out for washing clothes or such. Besides, the wind is too strong today. Nothing would stay on the lines. You said you don't know how to make cheese or butter?"

I shook my head.

"Can you bake bread?" he asked this with one eyebrow raised, as if daring me to fall short in this most basic of matronly skills.

"It's been a while, but I did learn when I was a girl." The superiority in my voice made me cringe slightly.

"My first wife, Dorothy," and here he paused to clear his throat and look away, "baked bread every three or four days. She usually made two loaves. Of course, that was back when Lucy was little more than a baby and Joseph wasn't eating solid food yet."

I tamped down my temper at this reminder of their too-recent tragedy and tried to resurrect that bud of compassion from the wagon ride. "I'll be sure to bake bread today. Is there anything else you think I should do?"

"Well, Emma knows what to do to make butter. Would you please show ... her how?" Jim asked his daughter, stumbling over what the children would call me.

"Yes, Pa," Emma replied dutifully.

Then Joseph spilled his milk and Jim barked at him, which set the boy off crying. Their father left soon after. I had spilled milk to clean, dishes to wash, and three children to mind, one of whom was wailing loudly.

It set us up for a long day. The crying and arguing crashed in never-ending waves over the soddy throughout the morning. I struggled to keep the fire burning at an even temperature and turned out four loaves of half-burnt, half-undercooked bread while I failed to maintain peace. My third attempt at baking bread was a modicum of success and, in exhaustion, I let the loaves clatter to the table to cool.

Then the butter-making lesson began. I was glad that Emma did, in fact, know what to do. She instructed me with an obnoxious attitude, however, and by the time I started churning, my patience and good humor were long gone. With arms already tired from kneading so much bread, I began the long, repetitive process of churning.

"Emma, go play with your brother," I found myself barking. "Lucy, stop that, he doesn't like it! If he's crying, stop doing it! Emma, I said play with him, not annoy him! Joseph, I can't take you to the outhouse right now. Emma, please take him. Fine, take over churning then and I'll take him. I don't care if you want to or not, get over here and churn this butter or, so help me, I will turn you over my knee and paddle you!"

Finally, the two younger children were fed lunch and put to bed for a nap and Emma was sent out to find her father with his lunch. I sank onto a bench and dropped my head onto my arms on the table. All my complaints from the previous night welled up and I gave in to a good cry.

Once the tears subsided, I felt better. It was like a hot summer day that is cooled by a sudden, severe rainstorm. Yes, I was not in an ideal situation. However, I wasn't defeated. The children had responded well to my silliness that morning. Clearly, they didn't like being yelled at. If I could keep my own emotions in check, I might be able to turn things around.

I got up from the table and searched the soddy. There were no toys and no books. I did uncover a stack of hand-written recipe cards, for which I was eternally grateful. I flipped through them, reading the ingredients and instructions hungrily. It was surprising how much I missed the books I'd read at the bookstore where I'd worked until my ill-advised rendezvous became cause to terminate my employment. There had been many stolen minutes with a novel in my hand and, now that I didn't have the luxury of so many books, I missed them dreadfully.

There was a recipe for oatmeal cookies and I found that I had all the necessary ingredients. I started mixing and measuring and once Emma arrived back at the soddy I was able to convince her to help me spoon out the dough onto the lone cookie pan. I wouldn't go so far as to say that we had a pleasant time, but there were entire stretches in which she didn't glare at me at all. Her little brow was furrowed in concentration as she carefully made each cookie the same size. This was a serious little girl, and I knew where she got that trait from.

The younger children awakened to the delicious aroma of freshly-baked cookies and each was happy to have a cup of milk and a pair of cookies. I showed them how to dunk the cookies in milk. Lucy immediately followed my lead and echoed my moans of delight once she tasted it. Joseph needed help the first time, but soon mastered the technique.

"I don't like cookies in my milk," Emma announced defiantly.

Lucy rolled her eyes. "Try it, Emma, you'll like it."

"No, I won't," the nine-year-old stubbornly insisted.

"That's all right," I stepped in. "Maybe Emma doesn't like delicious things." It was a low blow, but I couldn't help myself.

"Fine," Emma huffed. "I'll do it. But I won't like it."

She then dipped the tiniest corner possible into her milk and put the bite into her mouth. An exaggerated coughing fit ensued, which made her siblings' eyes grow wide. Once she could gasp for breath again, Emma gulped her milk.

"How did you like it?" I asked dryly.

I received a glare in response. Lucy's eyes looked to me, seeming to ask my permission to still like cookies dipped in milk. In response, I dipped my cookie back in my milk and took a big bite. "Oh, yum, that is so delicious!"

"Delicious," Lucy said. She nodded her head once decisively and followed my lead.

"'Licious," Joseph echoed and promptly dropped the remaining half of his cookie into his cup. He looked up at the rest of us and said, "Uh-oh," then burst into peals of laughter.

We three girls started our own round of giggles as the little boy fished his floating cookie out of his cup and ate it with dripping fingers. Even Emma dipped her cookie into her milk after that. I didn't say anything to draw attention to it, but I felt like I'd won a minor victory.

CHAPTER 4

AFTER OUR SNACK, I BUNDLED JOSEPH AND LUCY UP AND let them out to play in the yard. Emma assured me that the two knew to stay close to the house and away from anything dangerous. I suppose she was feeling generous, because Emma then went on to show me how to press the butter into the molds and we took them to the pantry to set. Her good deeds done for the day, she then left me to wash the churn in the cold and went to annoy her siblings. By the time the churn was as clean as I could make it, Joseph was holding my skirt, crying, and Lucy was screaming at Emma.

Back in the house we went. Supper was still a long way off, so I added a log to the fire and made up a long story about three children who found a magic carpet and flew through the sky. I suggested they sit on the bed and pretend it could take them anywhere.

"Where would we go?" Emma asked, staring at me blankly.

Did she really have no imagination? Or had they no idea of all the things out in the world, having grown up in this desolate place?

I gave up my hopes of writing Simon a letter and joined them on top of the quilt. "Look out! The bed's going up, up, into the sky. Careful! Don't fall off now, because it's a long way down."

Lucy giggled nervously and peeked over the side, not sure if she was willing to play the game along with me or not.

I leaned over the edge of the bed dramatically, "We're so high up!" I pulled myself back quickly and covered my eyes. "I can't look! Lucy, are you brave enough to look?"

The little girl nodded eagerly, her smile wide. She stood and walked to the foot of the bed, where she timidly craned her neck.

"Aren't we so very high in the sky?" I asked.

"Yes!" she cried in excitement.

At that point, Joseph caught the thread of the game and clapped his hands happily before rolling right off the bed.

"Oh, no," Emma groaned, sure that the game would come to an end.

Joseph began to cry from his place outside of our imaginings.

"That's okay," I whispered. "Get back up here, Joey."

He jumped up, uncertainty on his face, arms up. I pulled him back up. "Should we go to the jungle, where we might see a lion? Or to the desert, where there's only sand as far as you can see? Or should we go back in time to Camelot and find some dragons?"

In the end, we visited all those places. I described them as vividly as I could. Three children growing up in the middle of the prairie with no books to read would have little chance of knowing about everything there was to see in the world. I left them on their own, praying that they would continue the game while I flipped a big stack of pancakes.

"Oh, no!" Emma cried. "It's the dragon again! Lucy, get Joseph to safety while I fight him off!"

I grinned to myself. While the pretend world continued behind me, I thought up a wonderful idea. Wouldn't it be fun to have a picnic on the floor? We could continue the magic carpet game while we ate. Surely even stern Jim would enjoy watching his children so animated and lively and not crying.

Within ten minutes, the game fell apart. Joseph kept insisting on getting off the bed to come and babble to me in his mostly-incoherent baby talk. Each time he climbed down, his sisters would groan loudly, Emma insisting that he was ruining everything. Then Lucy stopped following her sister's every order, which made Emma angry.

Destruction was imminent, so I stepped in.

"We're going to do something special for supper. Who wants to help?" As I had hoped, three hands shot into the air, all anger dissolving immediately.

Soon I had one of the older blankets spread out and plates, cups, and utensils were laid out. The plate of pancakes was brought over, along with a jar of maple syrup, and some fried sausages that filled the house with their tempting scent. Milk was poured for the children and coffee for me.

I decided it was better to start the children on their supper than to wait for Jim, who might come at any time. So, I asked Lucy to say Grace and we dug in. In between bites, I told them about the far-off country of China where they had built a wall that was so long, it would take weeks to walk from one end to the other.

"Wow," Emma breathed, blinking in concentration. "How do you get to China … What are we supposed to call you?"

I was taken aback by the question. I hadn't come up with an answer for that myself and wasn't sure if Jim had an opinion or not. "I'm not sure," I admitted.

"You're not our mother," Emma said fiercely.

Understanding the importance of that statement, I nodded solemnly. "I would never try to take the place of your mother. She was a very special person to all of you."

Lucy's lower lip quivered slightly. Tears were looming, when Joseph stuck a sticky finger in his eye and started laughing, which got the rest of us laughing, too.

"What about Miss Betsy?" I suggested, before realizing that I wasn't a miss at all anymore.

But, Emma didn't like the name anyway. "You could be Aunt Betsy. We call one of Mama's friends Aunt Mabel, even though she isn't really our aunt."

I considered it. "Would it be confusing to call me Aunt when I'm married to your father?"

Lucy didn't have an opinion, but she was watching intently, her dress pulled over her knees and tucked under her toes, which were wiggling in anticipation. Joseph pretended to stick himself in the eye again and let out a few halfhearted giggles to see if he could make us laugh again. When he was roundly ignored, he went back to shoveling gooey bites into his mouth.

"It might be," Emma agreed.

"Maybe," I said slowly, not sure how the idea would go over, "we could find a name that means mother but isn't one that you would have used for your real mother. You called her mama, right?"

Emma nodded, brow furrowed. I was on thin ice.

"Well, in France they call their mothers *mere.*"

"That sounds like a horse." Emma's face twisted into distaste.

I chuckled. "I guess it does."

"What do they call mothers in China?" Lucy asked in a small voice.

"That's a good question, Luce. I don't know. I've never met someone from China to ask." I reached over and ran a hand over her silky blonde curls.

"Do you know any other countries?" asked Emma.

So my idea might work after all. I grabbed onto her

seeming approval with gusto. "In Germany, they call their mothers *mutter*."

"Mutter!" Emma burst into giggles. Lucy joined her a beat later, not quite understanding what was so funny.

I smiled at them. "In England, they call their mothers *mum*."

"Mum?" Emma tried it out.

"Mum!" Joseph shrieked.

"What do you think? Should I be called Mum?" I asked.

"All right. We'll call you Mum," Emma decided just as the door opened and Jim walked in.

He towered over us, boots caked with frozen mud. He pushed the door shut behind him and took in all of us sitting on the blanket, supper mostly finished.

"What are you doing?" His voice was tense, and the camaraderie from moments earlier disappeared.

It was my turn to feel defiant. "We thought that having a picnic on the floor would be such fun. And we were having a wonderful time, weren't we?"

Lucy was doing a good imitation of a turtle by trying to pull her shoulders up to her ears, eyes wide. Emma was studiously ignoring me and eating her food as though she had no part in the tomfoolery that was going on. Joseph was no help either, since I realized he was now wearing syrup from his forehead to his elbows.

"Get up to the table," Jim commanded.

I got to my feet and stood in front of him, having to tilt my head back to see his face. "I need to talk to you outside." I brushed past him and stepped out into the cold wind.

By the time I turned around to face him, Jim was already telling me what I'd done wrong. "My family does not eat on the ground like animals!"

I put up a hand to stop what was sure to be a tirade. "Did you spend the entire day with your children?" I asked as calmly as I could, though I was beginning to hum with the thrill of an argument.

"No," he conceded, and kicked at the dirt.

"Well, I did. I had to wipe noses and bottoms all day. I had to stop fights and dry tears. There are no toys, books, or other children to play with in this house. On top of that, it's too cold for them to play outside for long. Now, if you want me to keep my sanity, you are going to have to allow me to entertain your children the way that I know how." My hands were on my hips and I'm pretty sure Jim took a small step back by the end of my tirade.

He ran a hand roughly through his thick, curling hair. "I don't like them eating on the floor."

"Why not, for heaven's sake?" I asked, throwing my hands up. "They were having a good time."

"I built that table so they could be civilized. I don't want them to be wild savages just because they're growing up in the middle of nowhere."

I nodded. "I don't want that either. But I also want them

to have a chance to imagine things and to laugh. Every time you came in today, all the laughter drained from the room."

Jim's eyes met mine with a flash. "You don't know how hard it's been, Betsy! I've had to handle everything here. The farm, the house, the children, all of it! Ever since my Dorothy died, I've had to do it all."

My hands rose defensively. "You're right; I don't know how hard that must have been for you. I'm sure it was a very heavy weight on your shoulders."

"It was," he nodded, his clenched jaw the only evidence of his deep emotions.

"But you're not alone anymore. I'm here now." I searched his face and read only deep sorrow. "Things won't be the same as when your wife was alive; we both know that. Maybe, if you let me, we can start a new chapter for this family. Maybe we can all find a way to live together and maybe we'll find a way to be happy someday."

Jim shook his head slowly then turned and walked off towards the soddy dugout he'd made to house the animals and called "the barn." His shoulders were hunched and his hands were in his pockets, the very picture of defeat. I sighed and turned back to the warmth of the house where the children were waiting with wide eyes.

I had the dishes washed and the children in bed by the time Jim appeared. I was perched on the bed, leaning against the wall with Joseph in my lap, Lucy pressed against my side, and Emma just far enough away to hear my words but not give the impression of allegiance. We were singing "Frere Jacques," which I'd taught them. Emma was careful to copy my accent and seemed to delight in the foreignness of the words. Lucy was mostly making up her own words from the sounds and Joseph was snuggled sleepily against me with his thumb in his mouth and his other hand tugging his ear.

"We left you a plate on the warmer," I said once Jim had hung up his coat. He nodded and took his plate to the table.

"Mum, where's France?" Emma asked primly.

"Remember how I told you about England? Well, England is across the ocean from us and France isn't too far away."

"Is it near China?" Lucy's sleepy voice piped up.

"No, they're both very far away from China." I glanced up to see Jim following this exchange closely. "If you three promise to lie quietly, I'll tuck all three of you into the big bed until your father and I get ready for sleep."

This was deemed a good plan. With only a minor disagreement over who had to lie next to the wall and who got to sleep next to Joseph, the three were soon tucked snugly under the blankets and kissed good night.

I turned and walked over to the table, bringing the lamp with me.

"You're right," Jim said without preamble.

"That's a first," I replied dryly, managing to wring a crooked smile from my husband.

"You have a good way with the kids. I need to let you run the house the way you see fit."

I could see what those words cost him. "If you don't mind my asking, what was Dorothy like?"

Jim took a deep breath then blew it out, not meeting my eyes. Finally he said huskily, "She was tall and thin with brown hair."

"Like Emma," I nodded.

Jim looked over at where his daughter slept. "I suppose so, though she acts more like me than her ma."

"Oh?" I prompted.

"Dorothy was a dreamer. It was her idea that we come here to find good land for a farm." Jim's eyes took on a faraway look. "The land where we were was tired and there were a lot of farmers around. It drove the price up of land too high for us to ever buy a farm of our own. Then Dorothy read about how the government was giving land away to people who would settle in Oklahoma. She had it all planned out before I could even understand what she was saying."

He chuckled and scratched his bearded chin. "Of course, Oklahoma wasn't what she'd planned." Jim threw a glance over his shoulder to see if the children were listening. He went on quietly, just in case. "I built the best house I could, but it wasn't the house she'd imagined. Life out here is hard. I don't think Dorothy was able to cope with the wind and the solitude."

I got up to refill our coffee cups then sat down, hands wrapped around my warm mug. "What happened?"

Jim took a sip and sighed. "She just wasn't the same after Joseph was born. It wasn't a hard birth. At least, not any worse than the girls' had been. But there weren't any neighbors around to lend a hand afterward. Dorothy couldn't seem to see the good in life any more. Finally, she stopped getting out of bed. No matter what I did, she just laid there."

He was staring blankly at the table, seeing something from the past. I knew the Tuckers had lost their mother, but I hadn't realized it had been quite so grim.

"She got a bad cold at first. Since she wouldn't get up anymore, it was easy for pneumonia to set in. She got sick faster than I would have thought possible. And then she was just gone." Jim sat in silence for a long minute and I couldn't find the words to break into his reverie. Finally, he cleared his throat and his eyes met mine. "It's getting late. I should get to bed."

I nodded and said that I'd visit the outhouse once more. I wrapped a shawl around my shoulders and stepped out into the night. The constant wind was a low whine and the cold air found all the thin spots of my clothing. It would be easy to lose hope in such a desolate place. Before stepping back into the warm soddy, I whispered a prayer that I wouldn't fall prey to the prairie.

CHAPTER 5

LIFE CONTINUED ON THE FARM THROUGH THE REST OF the winter and into the spring. Some days dragged on as though they would never end, while others flew by. We fell into some habits that helped us all. Before the winter had given up its seemingly interminable hold on the land, Lucy and Joseph were as pleasant and friendly as I could have hoped for. They still cried and whined and irritated each other, of course, but they also were quick to hug me or snuggle up on my lap. When I had to discipline them, they were able to get back to their cheerful selves after the sting of a scolding had worn off.

Emma was a horse of a different color. There were times when I thought we were on good terms and we laughed and talked a bit. But one wrong word from me and she was back to glaring at me and picking at her siblings whenever my back was turned. I swore that girl was going to give me gray hair and wrinkles before I had a chance to turn twenty. We had our good days and our bad days and never seemed to make much progress beyond that.

Jim was entirely different, too. After our first evening talk at the table, we fell into a pattern of sharing one last cup of coffee and chatting quietly for a few minutes after the kids were in bed. It was comfortable and easy. He was never one to smile or laugh much. I suppose the weight of the farm and his family sat too heavily on his shoulders. He was also never one to pry, for which I was very grateful. Jim asked how the day had been, how the children had behaved, how well the supplies were holding out, but never about my life before the farm. I got the impression that he was waiting for me to be ready to share that information.

It was nice not to have to think about my life in North Carolina. My thoughts were full of the children and the house. It began to feel funny to remember that there had once been a time in which I'd had the spare time to flirt and date and go to supper parties. I'd loved my life back in Raleigh, but this new life was so much more significant that the two didn't really compare. It was like asking if I preferred cake or the color blue. During the day I was so busy I didn't have time to think about much of anything. At night, though, I found myself dreading the next fifty years spent in this same soddy doing the same things. How would I bear it?

I did finally get a letter written to Simon and mailed when we went to town for supplies. He was the one thing from my former life that I wasn't able to shake loose. I was loved by Lucy and Joseph, tolerated by Emma, and appreciated by Jim. Still, it didn't compare with being adored by Simon. I replayed our time together on the train in my mind almost every night as I lay next to Lucy and waited for sleep to come. What would have happened if we'd been able to meet when we were free of obligations? We would have married and started a life together, surely. As the days turned to weeks, I built an elaborate dream home in my mind. Since there was no chance of it ever being a reality, it felt like a harmless pastime.

"ARE YOU READY TO GO?" JIM ASKED, HIS HEAD JUST inside the door.

I finished lacing Joseph's boot and called, "Almost! Lucy and Emma are ready. You can take them out while I finish with Joey."

I glanced over my shoulder to catch Jim's pointed look of disapproval at my nickname for his son. I knew he wasn't fond of it and couldn't seem to resist teasing him about it whenever I could. I counted it as the final whimper of my flirtatious nature, which I was sure was dying with no one to practice on.

Before long, we were in the wagon and setting off to Guthrie. The children were in high spirits and I couldn't blame them. Now that the spring planting was done, Jim had decided we could go to town to refill our stores and get a change of view. I had trouble sitting still on the bench myself, to tell you the truth.

"Is that the empty farm you were telling me about?" I asked Jim, pointing off to the west.

"Yep, that's the one. The farmer couldn't keep up with the crops and gave up a year before the land would have been his." Jim shook his head regretfully. "It's been long enough now that it'll be hard to sell. A new owner will have a struggle getting it going again."

"How much longer before you own your farm?"

"Actually, it was seven years at the beginning of the month." Jim looked proud.

I gave his arm a light smack. "You should have told me! I could have baked a cake and we could have had a celebration."

"It wasn't any big thing." My husband shook his head. "You just want any excuse to make a fuss."

He wasn't wrong. In the eight weeks that I'd lived with the Tuckers, I'd found cause for three picnics, four cakes, and one pancake-eating contest. The children were always thrilled and even Jim had come to accept that he might come home to a festive atmosphere at any time.

"Do you think you'll live here always?" I asked. It was hard to imagine that Jim was the sort of man who dreamed of the future or even thought of much other than his mundane life.

"I don't know," he said slowly. "It's been seven years and I feel like I know the land pretty well by now. It's hard to believe that I'll live the rest of my life without any trees in sight, though."

We rode along in the quiet for a few minutes. I picked at the fraying edge of my coat sleeve and looked out at the never-changing landscape, feeling inexplicably glum.

"You should have a new coat," Jim said suddenly.

I smiled at him a little sadly. "That would be nice. I've had this one for a long time. I must have been about fourteen when my grandmother made it for me. Coats last many years in North Carolina since we don't wear them nearly as long as you do out here."

"Order one today at the store."

I looked up at Jim in surprise. He wasn't the type to make jokes, but this was such a generous offer that I was afraid to take him at his word. "Do you mean it?"

"Sure," he shrugged. "That coat is frayed and won't keep you warm enough for the deep cold of our winter days."

"Thank you," I said in a voice barely above a whisper. Never before had I experienced such kindness from a man. In fact, it had been a long time since I'd received a gift without any expectation of reciprocation. I couldn't help but feel my heart warm a bit towards my husband.

Lucy began to whine about her brother from the back of the wagon and any chance at adult conversation was ruined. I tucked Jim's words away, hoping that they meant that there might still be another adventure awaiting us somewhere along the line.

We sang and told stories the rest of the way to town. I was starting to go hoarse by the time we reached the edges of town and the children were too excited to listen to me. Jim and I shared a smile at their cries of delight. The wagon pulled to a stop near the livery and Jim helped us all down.

"Go on up to the general store and I'll meet you there," he ordered.

"Which of you wants to go with your father?" I asked. I knew Jim would get more done without a small child to look after, but then, so would I.

Ignoring his reproachful glare, it was soon decided that I would take Lucy and the other two would go with Jim. Before he could mount a defense, I took the little girl's hand and sailed off down the street. Lucy was busy looking all around her and I took advantage of this to stop at the post office for the mail.

My heart pounded as I flipped through the small stack of letters. There was a catalog for farm tools, a letter from the homesteader office, two from friends back in North Carolina, and one in a decidedly masculine hand, addressed to me. I bit my lower lip as I turned the envelope around. It was from Corporal Simon Hart at Fort Laramie. I withheld a squeal of delight and tore the letter open.

My Dear Betsy,

I can't begin to tell you all the things I felt when I received your letter. I was so glad to see your handwriting and know that you were safe. It was agony, though, to read about your life as a married woman. I must confess, I've spent many pleasant hours dreaming of what might have been, had our circumstances been different.

I lifted a shaky hand to my lips and blinked away an onrush of tears. I checked to make sure that Lucy was otherwise engaged before turning my anxious eyes back to the letter. Simon went on to describe his daily life at Fort Laramie. He explained that it was a busy place with trappers coming and going. The native Indians around the fort weren't particularly ornery and gave them little trouble, for which I breathed a prayer of thanks.

Things will get even more hectic as the summer unfolds. Fort Laramie, I have learned, is a stop for almost all of the wagon trains going to Oregon. My fellow officers said that as many as forty wagon trains might come through in the course of a summer. So many settlers are headed to the rich soil and tall trees out West. The Homestead Act has won over many brave adventurers.

I caught my breath and my eyes widened, fixing on a point on the far wall. Going west to Oregon. Traveling to Fort Laramie. Brave adventurers. No, surely Jim wouldn't want to do anything as dangerous as travel across the country with three small children. But the farm was his now. He could sell it any time he wanted. And he wanted to see trees again. I read Simon's words about the good soil again.

Shaking my head, I tried to assure myself that this was nonsense. But as I filled the order for the supplies we needed at the general store, I couldn't stop my mind from going back to Simon's letter again and again. In fact, I was so distracted that I lost Lucy once and then had to stop myself from ordering more than twice the flour we would need.

It was a relief to meet up with Jim and the other children so that my brain would stop its whirling. Jim made arrangements to pick up the supplies later and then suggested we walk to the bakery for a treat.

"We should celebrate the farm finally belonging to us," he said with a shy smile.

I offered a shaky one in return and followed his lead down the street. My brain refused to follow the conversation and I ended up following Jim like an automaton through the bakery and off to find a spot to picnic.

"Is everything all right?" Jim's voice interrupted my thoughts.

I blinked up at him and nodded hastily, not sure what we'd been discussing. The children were playing in the town square, chasing each other around and around. The pie Jim had bought was now no more than crumbs in the tin.

"I received a letter today," I ventured. How could I bring this up without mentioning too much about Simon?

"Oh?" Jim leaned back on the grass, his long legs stretched out in front of him. "Bad news?"

I pulled my knees up to my chest. "No, nothing like that. It's just that my friend mentioned going west to Oregon and now I can't seem to get that thought out of my mind." I offered him an apologetic smile, in case he might need it.

Jim rolled onto his side, one hand under his head. "West to Oregon Territory? That's a thought."

"It would be too dangerous," I insisted, as though I wasn't seriously thinking about it. "Too far for the children to travel."

We sat in silence for a long moment.

"My friend did mention that the soil is rich and there are lots of trees," I couldn't help mentioning.

Jim looked up at me and raised an eyebrow.

"And the Homestead Act now allows settlers to claim land out there just like here. In seven years, you could own a farm with trees for building a big house and soil that would produce a better crop."

Jim looked over at where the children played. "Are there many people out there? Lots of towns nearby? It would be nice if the kids could go to school and have some friends not too far off."

"I don't know the specifics, but there are more than forty wagon trains going every summer. There must be many towns popping up all over the territory!" My heart was galloping again. Was Jim really considering this?

"It's funny you mention it," Jim squinted his eyes thoughtfully. "Bill Harris at the livery told me that the railroad was interested in buying land up our way. Maybe we could sell the farm and head west. Maybe ..."

I wanted to jump up and cheer. Leave the ceaseless winds of the plains? Find a new place to live where there might be other people nearby? New friends and neighbors? Suddenly the monotonous life I'd pictured with the Tuckers was evolving into something new and exciting.

"I guess I could look into it. Do you want to go to Oregon?" Jim's eyes found mine.

"Yes," I said staunchly. There were dozens of reasons not to go, but I refused to consider them any further.

My husband nodded slowly. "Coming here was Dorothy's dream and it didn't turn out the way we'd hoped. It's been a sad place for us for a long time." He mulled things over for another few minutes while my fingers were crossed in my lap. Then he sat up and said, "Let's go to Oregon, Betsy."

I could have kissed him! That thought was a strange intrusion into the moment and I ended up smiling awkwardly at him instead, pushing the idea of kissing Jim Tucker out of my mind forcefully.

The ride back to the farm was filled with our excited plans for getting the farm ready to sell, supplying the wagon, and traveling to a jumping off point. There were too many things to speculate about to have a clear picture of what the next weeks would bring, but we had such fun hoping and wondering.

It wasn't until I was in bed and the house was quiet that I allowed my heart to give in to the real reason I was thrilled to go west: Simon Hart. I didn't know what would happen when we saw each other again. I didn't dare to dream of our little cabin in the woods since it would mean leaving the Tuckers and going back on my wedding vows. I wouldn't leave the children, I wouldn't. I would see Simon again and enjoy his company for a few hours before returning to my life with my new family.

Wouldn't I?

To continue enjoying Oregon Trail Complete Series

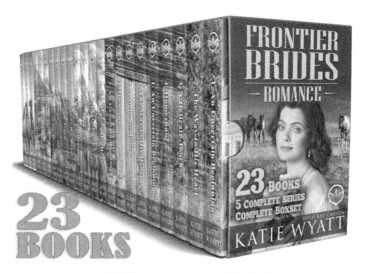

Frontier Brides Romance 23 Books 5 Complete Series

THANK YOU SO MUCH FOR READING MY BOOK. I SINCERELY hope you enjoyed every bit reading it. I had fun creating it and will surely create more.

YOUR POSITIVE REVIEWS ARE VERY HELPFUL TO OTHER reader, it only takes a few moments. They can be left at Amazon.

https://www.amazon.com/Katie-Wyatt/e/B011IN7AF0

WANT FREE BOOKS EVERY WEEK? WHO DOESN'T!

BECOME A PREFERRED READER AND WE'LL NOT ONLY SEND you free reads, but you'll also receive updates about new releases.

SO YOU'LL BE AMONG THE FIRST TO DIVE INTO OUR LATEST new books, full of adventure, heartwarming romances, and characters so real they jump off the page.

IT'S ABSOLUTELY FREE AND YOU DON'T NEED TO DO anything at all to qualify except go to.

PREFERRED READ FREE READS

HTTP://KATIEWYATTBOOKS.COM/READERSGROUP

ABOUT THE AUTHOR

KATIE WYATT IS 25% AMERICAN SIOUX INDIAN. BORN and raised in Arizona, she has traveled and camped extensively through California, Arizona, Nevada, Mexico, and New Mexico. Looking at the incredible night sky and the giant Saguaro cacti, she has dreamed of what it would be like to live in the early pioneer times.

Her books are a mixture of actual historical facts and events mixed with action and humor, challenges and adventures. The characters in Katie's clean romance novels draw from her own experiences and are so real that they almost jump off the pages. You feel like you're walking beside them through all the ups and downs of their lives. As the stories unfold, you'll find yourself both laughing and crying. The endings will never fail to leave you feeling warm inside.